SHARKY McSHARK

and the Teensy Wee Crab

For Matthew, Riley,
Rudi and Max
xxxx
A.M.

ORCHARD BOOKS

First published in Great Britain in 2020 by The Watts Publishing Group

10 9 8 7 6 5 4 3 2 1

Text and illustrations © Alison Murray 2020

A CIP catalogue record for this book is available from the British Library.

ISBNs: HB 978 1 40835 828 3   PB 978 1 40835 829 0

Printed and bound in China

Orchard Books
An imprint of Hachette Children's Group
Part of The Watts Publishing Group Limited
Carmelite House, 50 Victoria Embankment, London EC4Y 0DZ

An Hachette UK Company
www.hachette.co.uk   www.hachettechildrens.co.uk

SHARKY McSHARK

and the Teensy Wee Crab

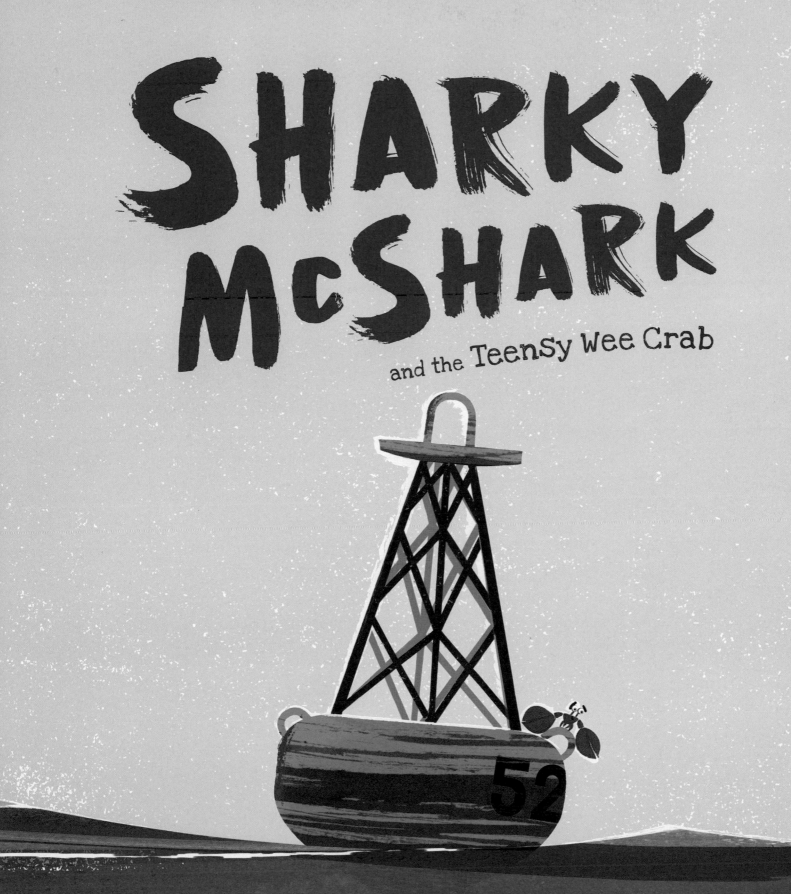

Alison Murray

ORCHARD

Down at the bottom of
the deep, blue sea lived the
meanest, most fearsome
creature that had ever swam
in the watery depths.
Sharky McShark
was her name.

When Sharky
was around,
the clownfish
cleared out,

Pa! You clowns
taste funny!

the
flatfish fled,

Back in your
plaice, flatties!

and even the rocks
got out of her way.

Aha - Sharky always eats
her CRUST-aceans!

Sharky was the biggest bully
in the sea. She had no friends
and she didn't want any.

Being a lone shark was best,
she thought to herself.
I don't need a sole.

Puffers are
duffers!

Then, one day, out of nowhere . . .

PLONK!

a teensy wee crab bounced off Sharky's fin, nipped her nose and landed on the seabed in front of her.

"Who dares nip my nose?" said Sharky McShark. "I will eat you right up."

Oops! Sorry!

The teensy wee crab quivered with fear. "Please don't eat me!" she cried. "Spare my life and I promise I'll return the favour. You never know when YOU might need MY help."

Well, Sharky McShark found that VERY funny. "Help?" she sneered. "From a teensy wee thing like YOU?!"

HA HA!

Sharky laughed . . .

HAHAHAHAHAHA!

and laughed
and laughed.
HA HA HA HA HA

HA HA!

She laughed SO hard
that she tumbled backwards
into an old fishing net . . .

that was tangled
on the hook of a rusty
anchor . . .

that was attached to an
ancient wreck . . .

that was balanced
on the edge
of a
deep sea abyss.

For the first time
in a hundred years,
the old ship
creaked
into life . . .

then down it fell

into the deep, deep dark,

dragging Sharky with it.

Lying
at
the
bottom
of the
deep,
dark abyss,
Sharky
McShark
was
no longer
the
meanest . . .

or the most
fearSome creature
in the sea . . .

she was the
loneliest.

"I wish someone would come to
my rescue," she said. "I wish I had . . .
a friend."

And then, as if a thousand lightbulbs
had come on in her mind, Sharky realised.
"I'm a bully because I'm scared . . .

Scared that no one
will like me."

Now I'll never have a friend,
thought Sharky McShark.

Then, all of a sudden, out of nowhere . . .

PLINK! PLANK! PLONK! Someone familiar bounced off Sharky's nose and landed on the seabed in front of her.

The teensy wee crab set about snipping and snapping, clipping and cutting, until at last . . .

Sharky
was free!

And right then and there,
she decided to do the
biggest, **bravest** thing
she had ever done . . .

"Will you be my friend?"
She asked.

"Of course!" said the teensy wee crab, who knew that even big, bad bullies deserve a second chance.

And as it turned out . . .

Sharky McShark
was no longer
the meanest,
most fearsome
creature in the
deep, blue sea . . .

she was the
friendliest.

Best fins for ever!